GET OUT ALIVE!

ESCAPE FROM THE
SPOTTED ASSASSIN

Julie K. Lundgren

CHERRY LAKE PRESS

Published in the United States of America by Cherry Lake Publishing Group
Ann Arbor, Michigan
www.cherrylakepublishing.com

Reading Adviser: Beth Walker Gambro, MS, Ed., Reading Consultant, Yorkville, IL

Photo Credits:
© Efimova Anna/Shutterstock, cover, (cheetah), © Photography Phor Phun/Shutterstock, cover, (springbok), and page 19, (top), © klyaksun/Shutterstock (graphic on cover and throughout book); © Cassette Bleue/Shutterstock, speech bubbles throughout; © Nazarkru/Shutterstock, yellow bursts throughout; background illustration used throughout book © Melinda Raduly/Shutterstock; © Tony Campbell/Shutterstock, page 3; © TJ Travel/Shutterstock, page 4; © Volodymyr Burdiak/Shutterstock (top 3 cats), © Miguel Schmitter/Shutterstock (cubs), © brunodesimoni/Shutterstock (inset), page 5; © Wayne Marinovich/Shutterstock (cheetah), © RuskaPixs/Shutterstock, page 6; © Franck Legros/Shutterstock (top), © photobar/Shutterstock, page 7; © Beate Wolter/Shutterstock, (duiker), © rawf8/Shutterstock, steenbok, © Robert Harding Video/Shutterstock, (gazelle), © PACO COMO/Shutterstock, (impala), page 8; © Pascal Vosicki/Shutterstock, page 9; © Stu Porter/Shutterstock, page 10; © Radzimy/Shutterstock, (top), © Chaithanya Krishnan/Shutterstock, © Rebius/Shutterstock, (inset), page 11; © Cathy Withers-Clarke/Shutterstock, page 12; © Torbjoern Lundqvist/Shutterstock, page 13; © Sam DCruz/Shutterstock, (top), © Henk Bogaard/Shutterstock, (wild dog), © Martin Mecnarowski/Shutterstock, (jackal), © Martin Pelanek/Shutterstock, (hyena), page 14; © Bildagentur Zoonar GmbH/Shutterstock, (top), © Jurgens Potgieter/Shutterstock, page 15; © Simon Eeman/Shutterstock, page 16 and page 23, (bottom); © Rolf Barbakken/Shutterstock, © Rita_Kochmarjova/Shutterstock, (inset), page 17; © Nigel Housden/Shutterstock, page 18; © Lasse Johansson/Shutterstock, (bottom), page 19; © Steve Allen/Shutterstock, (top and inset), page 20; © Bildagentur Zoonar GmbH/Shutterstock, page 21; © Elana Erasmus/Shutterstock, pages 22-23.

Produced for Cherry Lake Publishing by bluedooreducation.com

Copyright © 2026 by Cherry Lake Publishing Group

All rights reserved. No part of this book may be reproduced or utilized in any form or by any means without written permission from the publisher.

Library of Congress Cataloging-in-Publication Data has been filed and is available at catalog.loc.gov.

Printed in the United States of America

Note from Publisher: Websites change regularly, and their future contents are outside of our control. Supervise children when conducting any recommended online searches for extended learning opportunities.

ABOUT THE AUTHOR

Julie K. Lundgren grew up in northern Minnesota near Lake Superior. She delighted in picking berries, finding cool rocks, and trekking in the woods. She still does! Julie's interest in nature science led her to a degree in biology. She adores her family, her sweet cat, and Adventure Days

Contents

SPOT A KILLER 4
I AM A SUPER PREDATOR! 6
LEAPING TARGET 12
GET OUT ALIVE! 18
FIND OUT MORE 24
GLOSSARY 24
INDEX 24

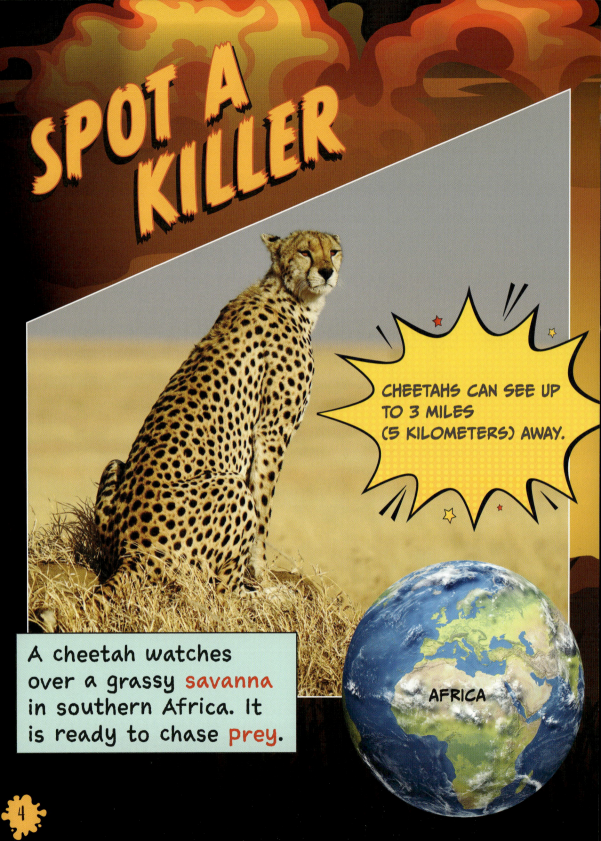

Cheetahs share the land with other big cats. Unlike them, cheetahs hunt during the day.

LEOPARD

LION

CHEETAH

Cheetah mothers give birth to two to six furry cubs. She must hunt to feed them.

A CHEETAH'S COLORS AND SPOTS HELP IT HIDE IN DRY GRASSES.

Cheetahs try to avoid fights with prey. They hunt animals that run for their lives.

DUIKER

STEENBOK

THOMSON'S GAZELLE

IMPALA

SWIFT RUNNERS LIKE THESE TWIST, TURN, AND LEAP TO ESCAPE PREDATORS.

Cheetahs must rest after a chase. Then they eat fast. They don't want to share with other hunters.

CHEETAH CLAWS STAB THE GROUND AS THEY RUN FOR EXTRA GRIP. THEY NEVER **RETRACT.**

To kill, cheetahs crush the prey's throat in their jaws. The prey cannot breathe. Cheetahs use their teeth to rip meat, not to kill.

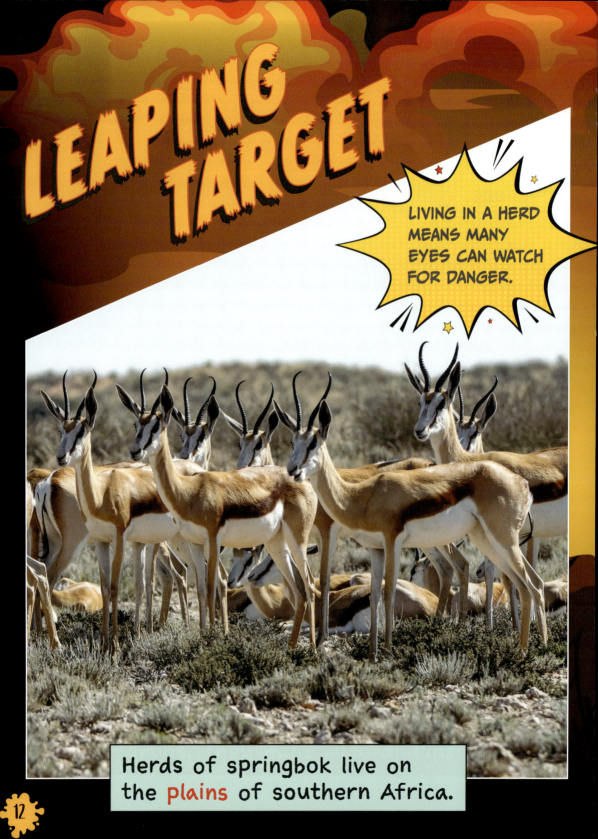

Springbok eat grasses, flowers, and shrubs. They get most of the water they need from plants.

A SPRINGBOK IS A KIND OF ANTELOPE.

Big cats hunt speedy springbok. Hyenas, wild dogs, and jackals eat this fast food too.

JACKAL

WILD DOG

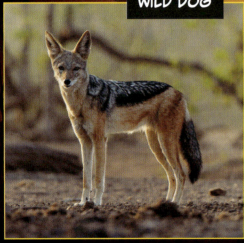

HYENA

The cheetah sees some springbok across the plains. She chirps to her cubs. She walks slowly and quietly toward the herd.

CHEETAH CUBS STAY WITH THEIR MOTHER FOR ABOUT 18 MONTHS. CHEETAH CUBS THEN STICK TOGETHER FOR A FEW MORE MONTHS UNTIL THEY CAN SURVIVE ALONE.

The cheetah creeps near. The herd is alert and nervous. Their long ears twitch.

SPRINGBOK HAVE EXCELLENT HEARING. THEY CAN HEAR TINY SOUNDS.

The cheetah suddenly appears! She runs into the herd. The springbok scatter.

The cheetah picks one springbok. The chase begins. The cheetah cannot keep up this high speed for long.

The springbok pivots. The cheetah still runs closer. The springbok pronks high above the hunter. It lands beyond the cheetah's claws. Escape!

Find Out More

Books

Meinking, Mary. *Cheetahs*, Lake Elmo, MN: Focus Readers, 2018

Chang, Kirsten. *Cheetah or Leopard?*, Minnetonka, MN: Bellwether Media, 2020

Websites

Search these online sources with an adult:

Cheetahs | National Geographic Kids
Springbok | Britannica

Glossary

alert (UH-lert) quick to notice danger

mammals (MAM-uhlz) animals that have hair and make milk to feed their young

plains (PLAYNZ) flat or rolling grasslands with few trees

predators (PRED-uh-terz) animals that hunt and eat other animals

prey (PRAY) animals hunted and eaten by other animals

pivots (PIH-vuhts) turns quickly from one direction to another

pronk (PRONK) to bounce straight up high into the air, with all four feet off the ground

retract (rih-TRAKT) to cover or draw back

savanna (suh-VAN-uh) a grassland with scattered trees and shrubs, usually with wet and dry seasons

spring (SPRING) a coil that can be pressed or pulled, then releases energy when the force is removed

strides (STRAHYDZ) takes long steps when walking or running

termite (TER-myte) insect that, with its colony, builds large dirt piles as homes

Index

big cats   5, 14
claws   11, 22
cubs   5, 19
eyes   12
grasses   5, 13
plains   12, 19
prey   4, 8, 10, 11, 18
pronk(s)   16, 17, 22
run(s)   8, 11, 15, 21
speed   7, 10, 16, 22
spots   5
spring   7